NO KISSES, PLEASE!

ISBN-13: 978-0-545-09891-5
ISBN-10: 0-545-09891-2

Copyright © 2004 by Hans Wilhelm, Inc.
All rights reserved. Published by Scholastic Inc.
SCHOLASTIC, CARTWHEEL BOOKS, NOODLES, and associated logos are trademarks
and/or registered trademarks of Scholastic Inc.
Lexile is a registered trademark of MetaMetrics, Inc.

10 9 8 7 6 5 4 3   9 10 11 12 13/0

Printed in the U.S.A.
This edition first printing, January 2009

 noodles™

NO KISSES, PLEASE!

by Hans Wilhelm

Alameda Free Library
1550 Oak Street

Cartwheel
·B·O·O·K·S·®

SCHOLASTIC INC.

New York   Toronto   London   Auckland   Sydney

Mexico City   New Delhi   Hong Kong   Buenos Aires

I hear a car!
We have a visitor.

Who can it be?

Oh, no.

It's Auntie Judy!

She always kisses me.

I hate kisses.
I must hide.

Now I am safe.

There you are.
I found you!

Oh, no!

HELLLLLP!

What should I do?

I have an idea!

I dig a hole.

Now you can kiss me.

It worked!
No kisses.

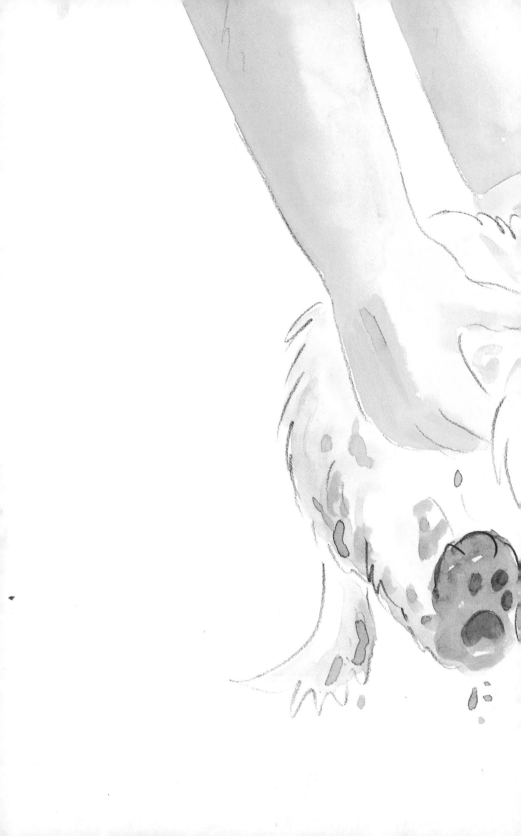

Oh, no. What now?

Baths are better than kisses.